I Never Did That Before

I Never Did That Before

poems by Lilian Moore

•

illustrated by Lillian Hoban

SCHOLASTIC INC.
New York Toronto London Auckland Sydney

For Will and Arkie
—L.M.

To Ilana
—L.H.

The text of this book is set in Univers Black
The illustrations are rendered in mixed media

ISBN 0-590-87211-7

12 11 10 9 8 7 6 5 4   7 8 9/9 0 1 2/0

Printed in the U.S.A.   09

First Scholastic printing, April 1997

TABLE of CONTENTS

Monkey Bars

Someone is climbing
the monkey
bars,
hand over
foot
foot over hand.

Someone's knees
hang over the
bar,

and the sky
is where
the ground
should be.

Someone is hanging
upside down
for the very first
time.

It's me!

New Sneakers

My new sneakers
want to
run.
They want to race
with every
one.

If I meet a rabbit
hopping by,
I'll cry, "Race you
to the corner!"
And I'll run run run.

If I pass a turtle,
slow and sedate,
I'll say, "Sorry
but I can't wait."
And I'll run run run.

If I see a puppy
looking for some fun,
I'll say,
"Let's play together!"
And we'll run run run.

Scary Bear

Each night
he's there
in the room
somewhere,
a hairy scary bear.

He comes at night
from far away,
from deep dark woods
where he lives
all day.

He snuffles and
growls
and when he prowls
around my
bed—
I slide
under the blankets
and cover my head.

Hey! He's not here
tonight.
No hairy bear in sight!
He's gone creeping to his
lair.
He knows I'm too big now
to scare.

Sour Pickle

My eyes are
teary bleary.
My tongue is
bee-sting hot.

I just bit
a pickle.
My mouth is all
a-prickle.

I'd rather
not
have anymore.

Pear Juice

Until you bite into
a pear
you cannot tell
how much there is
of sweet pear smell
within its skin,
or what a stream
of tickly juice
will
trickle
down
your
chin.

¡Hola, niño!

"¡Hola, niño!"
Mr. Santos greets me
when he meets me
in the street.

I never knew
what to say
before.

Now when he calls
"¡Hola, niño!"
I say "¡Hola, señor!"

Hola, niño (oh-la neen-yo): Hello, little boy
Hola, señor (oh-la sen-yor): Hello, sir

My Balloon

My balloon
    bobs beside me
    rides low
    on a string:
    a friendly thing.

Fat as a moon,
easy to
tease.
I really should not
squeeze
the soft stretchy skin,

but if I gave it
one more pinch
would it
　　slurp
　　swoosh
　　rumble
　　burp?

POP!

I miss my balloon.

Someone

The best kind of
grown-up to take
for a walk

is someone

who sees the sense
of peeking through a
fence,

who understands
you don't have to
hold hands,

who won't worry
if you don't hurry,

whom it won't disturb
if you walk the curb.

We took a nice walk
today,
Grandpa and I.

Best of All

I make believe
I can run
faster than a
deer.

I pretend
I can jump
way
to the moon.

I play
I can take
kangaroo hops
and never
fall.

But now that I have
learned to
skip,
I like that best
of all.

Blue and Yellow Mixing

I'm making a
picture.
I'm painting a house

and the roof
of my house is
pink.

The walls will be
yellow,
dandelion yellow,

and the windows
red,
I think.

Now I'm painting
blue on the
dandelion yellow

to give the
house a
door.

But the blue and
yellow
are
mixing

and the door is
turning
green.

Blue and
yellow making
green!

Have you ever
seen that
before?

Kittens

Our cat Arabella has
kittens,
tiny balls of fur.

One is coppery, one
is silvery,
two are white like her.

"Please may I touch a
kitten?" Arabella's
eyes say *no*.

"Please may I pet
a kitten?"
No, No—Not yet....

Soon the kittens
tumble
and bat their paws
in play.

"Please may I hold a
kitten?" *Yes, now
you may.*

I hold the coppery
kitten, and while
I stroke her fur,

she licks my chin with
rough pink tongue,
and I hear Arabella
purr.

Red Sled

On a red sled
one snowy day,
I rode down a hill
with the wind
all the way.

Over a hump and
over a bump and
    clear
        hill
           ahead!

Just me.
Just me
on a
red sled.

Big Brother

My big brother
calls me "Brat" and
"Tag-along" and
things like that,

but I don't care.
I like to go most
anywhere
with him.

"Well, Tag-along,"
he said today.
"Come along and
watch me play."

He let me wear his
baseball hat
and touch his very
special bat.

Then I held his
baseball mitt
and watched him bat a
three-base hit.

The Coat in My Closet

I opened the closet and
there was my coat—
the coat I wore last year.

"Your arms are too
long," said the sleeves,
very cross.

The zipper scolded, too.
"You're so wide now
I'll have to stop.

I'll never be able
to slide to
the top."

"I don't reach your knees,"
the coat complained.
"Whatever did you do?"

"Coat," I explained,
"I grew."